Little Fairy said,
"I wish for something **small** to eat."

So Sparkle waved her horn
to make a **tiny** strawberry treat.

Big, tall Giant said,
"I wish I had a **massive** snack."

So Sparkle swished her horn
to make the **largest** sandwich stack.

Fiery Dragon said,
"I wish for treats to **warm** me up."

So Sparkle twirled her horn
to make **hot chocolate** in a cup.

Snowy Yeti said,
"I wish for something very cold."

So Sparkle whirled her horn to make
a chilled ice cream to hold.

Sparkle felt a little **sad** now she was all alone.

She swirled her horn once more
to grant a wish all of her own...

In a flash, her friends appeared,
with special cupcakes too.

"Now I'm **happy,**" Sparkle said.
"My wishes have come true!"

Tear-Proof Books!

Unicorn's
Magical Wishes

Sparkle is a magical unicorn.
What wishes will she grant today?

Have fun pointing out the different opposites,
from big to small and hot to cold.
These special pages won't tear, and even
if they get chewed or messy, they can be
wiped clean, ready to be read again and again!

With illustrations by Dawn Machell

Copyright © 2020
make believe ideas ltd

The Wilderness, Berkhamsted, Hertfordshire, HP4 2AZ, UK.
501 Nelson Place, P.O. Box 141000, Nashville, TN 37214-1000, USA.

www.makebelieveideas.com
Written by Rosie Greening.

Parental Guidance

Read together

Includes opposites to encourage interaction

1+ YEARS

$4.99 U.S. $5.99 CAN

ISBN10: 1-78947-844-8
ISBN13: 978-1-78947-844-0

50499

9 781789 478440

12202002